DOCTOR·WHO

D0523902

THE DARKSMITH LEGACY

BBC CHILDREN'S BOOKS
Published by the Penguin Group
Penguin Books Ltd, 80 Strand, London, WC2R 0RL, England
Penguin Group (USA) Inc., 375 Hudson Street, New York 10014, USA
Penguin Books (Australia) Ltd, 250 Camberwell Road, Camberwell, Victoria 3124, Australia
(A division of Pearson Australia Group Pty Ltd)
Canada, India, New Zealand, South Africa
Published by BBC Children's Books, 2009
Text and design © Children's Character Books, 2009
This edition produced for The Book People Ltd,
Hall Wood Avenue, Haydock, St Helens, WA11 9UL
Written by Trevor Baxendale
Cover illustration by Peter McKinstry
1
BBC logo © BBC 1996. Doctor Who logo © BBC 2004. TARDIS image © BBC 1963.
Licensed by BBC Worldwide Limited.
BBC, DOCTOR WHO (word marks, logos and devices), and TARDIS are trademarks of the
British Broadcasting Corporation and are used under licence.
ISBN: 9781405906647
Printed in Great Britain by Clays Ltd, St Ives plc

DOCTOR · WHO

THE DARKSMITH LEGACY

THE GAME OF DEATH

BY TREVOR BAXENDALE

Book
6

The Darksmith adventure continues online. Log on to
the website, enter the special codes from your book
and enjoy games and exclusive content about
The Darksmith Legacy.

www.thedarksmithlegacy.com

Contents

The Story So Far...

The Doctor has taken the powerful Eternity Crystal from the terrible Darksmith Collective on the planet Karagula. The Crystal can create life, and the Doctor knows it mustn't be allowed to fall into the wrong hands.

Varlos, the Darksmith who created the Crystal, realized this too. He stole the Crystal and fled from Karagula. The Darksmiths need the Crystal to fulfil their commission for a mysterious client. The Darksmiths have sent a powerful robot Agent to recover the Crystal and kill Varlos and the Doctor.

Together with Gisella – a robot 'daughter' created by Varlos – the Doctor finds Varlos, who gives him a copy of the Crystal. But Varlos dies before he can tell the Doctor how to destroy the real Crystal. The Darksmiths' Agent tracks the Doctor and Gisella to Varlos' ship and the TARDIS...

Crash Landing

'What are you doing?' Gisella asked. 'Varlos didn't tell us how to destroy the Crystal.'

'No. But chances are the Agent knows how and where we could do it. And since he's got a lovely Darksmith ship right under his nose, he can head there now and try to stop us.' The Doctor grinned and flicked some switches on the TARDIS console. 'Not realizing that we will be following him. He'll lead us right to where we want to be!'

Gisella smiled. 'Doctor, that is extremely devious.'

'It is, isn't it!' the Doctor beamed. 'Aha! He's started the Darksmith engines. They'll just pop him through that little tear in reality and back out into local space...' He threw the take off lever and peered at the computer screen. 'We'll just wait for him in the Asteroid Belt, shall we? Look, here he comes...' But then the TARDIS lurched and shuddered. Sparks flew from the controls in a glittering shower. 'Oh, no...'

Gisella was thrown into the chair beside the console. 'What's happening?'

'Varlos must have left a trap for anyone wanting to follow his ship. He's charged his slipstream with destronic particles.'

'That doesn't sound good!' Gisella yelled over the rising roar of the TARDIS drive systems.

'A normal ship would burn up in a second.' The Doctor hung onto the console for dear life as the TARDIS spun and shook. 'Even with extrapolator shielding the particles will crack us open like an egg.'

'Then change course!'

'The controls are locked on.' He looked wildly at Gisella. 'If I can't get us free, we'll stay following that craft forever – in pieces!'

More sparks flew from the TARDIS controls in a glittering shower. The Doctor was hanging on for dear life now as the TARDIS tumbled through the Vortex, completely out of control.

'What's happening?' cried Gisella. She looked like a young, pretty girl with wide, dark eyes and black hair, but she was actually an extremely sophisticated android. She had been designed and built by a member of the Darksmith Collective, the galaxy's finest inventors. Gisella had joined the Doctor on his quest to destroy the ultimate weapon – the Eternity Crystal fashioned by the same Collective. But now Gisella found herself clinging onto the padded seats next to the TARDIS console while the Doctor struggled with the controls, wondering if this trip through time and space would be her last.

The TARDIS engines groaned in protest as the ship plunged on.

'We've been caught in a temporal slipstream,' the Doctor said.

Gisella had no time to ask him what that could possibly mean before he grabbed a mallet from the underside of the console and gave the controls a mighty whack. Suddenly the TARDIS stopped heaving like a ship at sea and settled down.

The Doctor's face broke into a huge grin. 'There we are,' he announced, 'never fails – when in doubt, hit it with a hammer!'

Cautiously, Gisella climbed down from the seat and approached the console. The Doctor was waving smoke away with one hand while he flicked switches and twisted dials with the other.

The Silver Devastation

An area of deep space where two galaxies collided over a hundred billion years ago. The resulting stellar collapse was called the Silver Devastation — a vast sector of space containing nothing but dead suns and dark matter. It was so-named as from a distance it looks like a huge silver sea hanging in space. The edge of the area is even referred to as its 'coast'.

It is a beautiful silver-coloured coruscation that has fascinated space travellers for millennia — drawing them from across the stars into the centre of a galactic maelstrom. There are endless rumours and myths surrounding the Silver Devastation. Some say it's populated by the mutant survivors of the two galaxies, or refugees from the Old Time caught in eternal conflict. Some say

there's nothing there but void – a bottomless chasm in time and space. Others say that it contains terrible, blood-sucking monsters from another universe entirely.

The legendary Face of Boe was said to be from the Silver Devastation, though its actual origins seem much older. Legends also tell of a child found naked on the coast of the Silver Devastation, with only a pocket watch. But such stories are probably just myths...

'Is it over?'

'What? Oh, that. Yeah, all done. The TARDIS and I know a thing or two about avoiding catastrophic time-space interstices.'

'You do?'

He nodded, but offered no further word of explanation.

The central glass column shone brightly, the internal filaments rising and falling. Gisella knew that this meant the TARDIS was still in flight. The Doctor was watching the hypnotic motion of the time rotor very closely, as if reading some significance in it as he made careful adjustments to the controls. 'Here we go,' he announced. 'Coming in to land...'

A raucous wheezing and groaning sound filled the room as the TARDIS began to materialize. Suddenly, the Doctor's cheery smile turned into an anxious frown.

'That can't be right,' he said as he grabbed the monitor screen and studied the readout.

'What's the matter?' Gisella asked.

'According to this we've materialized right in the middle of the Silver Devastation,' the Doctor said, frowning. He scratched his head in puzzlement.

'The TARDIS hung onto the Darksmith Agent's time trail without much difficulty – well, perhaps just a bit... all right, quite a lot of difficulty, actually – but these readings are all wrong. Very wrong. Wrong, wrong, wrong.'

'Why? What is the Silver Devastation, exactly?'

The Doctor grabbed his overcoat from a nearby stanchion. 'There are endless rumours and myths surrounding the Silver Devastation. Some say it's populated by the mutant survivors of the two galaxies, or refugees from the Old Time caught in eternal conflict. Some say there's nothing there but void – a bottomless chasm in time and space. Others say that it contains terrible, blood-sucking monsters from another universe entirely.'

Gisella eyed the TARDIS doors nervously. 'And we're about to go out there?'

The Doctor's solemn look switched instantly to one of cheery excitement. He grinned and winked at her. 'Oh, yes!'

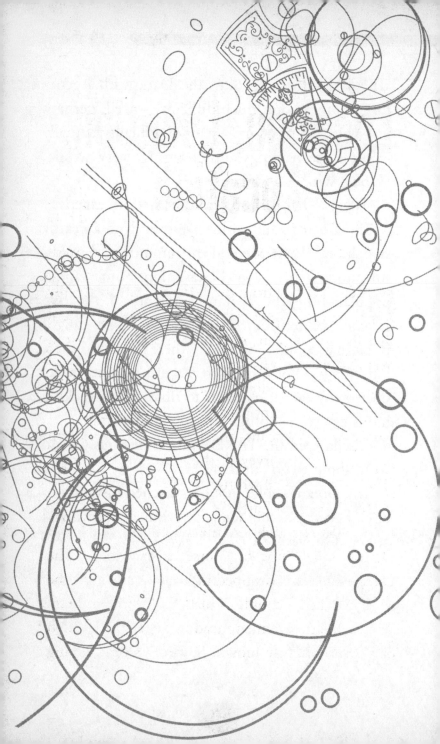

Location, Location, Location

Gisella stepped from the TARDIS, automatically checking to see that it had retained its usual disguise as an old blue police box from twentieth century Earth.

They were standing on a well cut lawn in the middle of an elegant garden.

'See what I mean?' the Doctor said, hands in pockets as he surveyed the tranquil landscape. 'Told you it was all wrong.'

'Are we still on Earth?'

'No. This is right in the middle of the Silver Devastation. Only, of course, it can't be...' The Doctor suddenly dropped to his haunches, felt the grass, plucked a couple of blades and sniffed them. 'Hmm, a rather refined meadow grass with a touch of Zoysia, recently mown. Someone's been taking care of the place, anyway.'

'And this place is...?'

'Impossible. That's what this place is.' The Doctor jumped up and strode off. He was heading for a nearby box hedge, meticulously trimmed, and a shade taller than he was.

Gisella hurried after him. They soon found a gap in the hedge – a graceful arch cut out of the foliage like a doorway. Stepping through, they found themselves standing by a gravel roadway and a line of tall coniferous trees.

'Poplars,' said the Doctor, walking off down the road. 'Always liked poplars. On the planet Cheem the trees can all talk. Isn't that brilliant? I wish all trees could talk. Imagine the tales they could tell.'

'These trees could have told us where we are,' smiled Gisella, joining in the fun.

'Precisely. Or we could just ask this old man. Hello!'

There was a man in an old flat cap and a waistcoat, pushing a wheelbarrow along the road. His shirtsleeves were rolled up and his hands were dirty.

He turned around at the Doctor's greeting. He had a kind, rather round face, with the ruddy complexion of someone who works outdoors all day long. 'Evenin',' he said, nodding his head. 'Which way did you come in, then?'

The Doctor pointed back at the hedge. 'That way.'

'Oh, right. You probably took a wrong turn.' The man chuckled warmly. 'Happens all the time around here. You should have come in the main entrance. I'm Ted, the gardener. The others are all up at the house.'

'Nice to meet you, Ted,' smiled the Doctor. He introduced himself and Gisella, and then said, 'What others?'

Ted laughed again. He seemed to find all this rather fun. 'What! You didn't think this was a private invitation, did you?'

'Er – no, of course not.'

Ted's jovial smile suddenly disappeared. 'Here – you have *got* an invitation, haven't you?'

The Doctor briefly showed him the piece of psychic paper in his wallet. It was enough to make the gardener think he had seen whatever kind of invitation he was expecting.

'Oh,' nodded Ted, relaxing. 'Well, I'd best be getting on, Doctor. The house is that way...' He pointed along the drive and smiled at Gisella. 'Have a nice time. Hope you're not the first to be killed!'

'I beg your pardon?' Gisella gaped.

'Well, y'know... I hope you manage to stay alive for a decent time. You look like a nice enough kid.'

'What are you talking about?' demanded the Doctor.

The gardener had gone quite pale. 'Well, sorry if I'm talking out of turn, sir... I don't mean to startle you. I've said more than enough, probably. I'd best be getting on...' The old man hesitated, biting his lip. 'Just be careful. That's all I can say.'

'Thanks,' said Gisella doubtfully. 'We will.'

'What an interesting gardener,' said the Doctor as Ted waved and continued on his way.

'What did he mean by that?' Gisella asked.

'Let's find out.'

They continued down the road, the Doctor frowning. Long shadows stretched across the lawns as the sun dipped behind the tree line and a cool breeze had sprung up seemingly from nowhere.

'Something isn't right here,' warned the Doctor as they walked. 'I mean, besides warnings from the local gardener about being killed. For a start, this entire place is impossible. There's no way any of this should be here. And there's no way anyone else should be here. And there's no way they should be inviting anyone else here either. Ah!'

They had turned a corner and found the house. It was an elegant country house, pale stone with lots of windows and a large, gravelled drive leading up to a wide entrance. The setting sun gave the house a warm, welcoming glow.

'It looks nice enough,' Gisella commented.

'Looks can be deceiving.'

'Are you always this suspicious?'

'What, of elegant country houses situated in their own grounds in the middle of a notorious region of interstellar destruction?' the Doctor paused as if considering, and then nodded. 'Yes, as a rule, I am.'

But that didn't stop the Doctor bounding up the steps to the large front doors and pointing to the doorbell. 'Go on, give it a go,' he urged Gisella.

It was a large brass handle hidden in a little stone alcove. Gisella reached out and gave it a sharp tug.

The Doctor was grinning again, despite his misgivings. 'I hope they've got the kettle on,' he whispered. 'I could murder a cup of tea.'

The doors opened and an imposing figure stared down at them. He was very tall, and completely bald – he didn't even have any eyebrows or eyelashes. He wore a sombre, old fashioned suit with a striped waistcoat.

'Good evening,' he said, 'although I should warn you that only half of that statement is true.' His voice sounded like the crunch of gravel beneath their feet. 'Welcome to Devastation Hall.'

'Lovely place,' said the Doctor. 'Very cosy. I'm the Doctor and this is Gisella. I believe we're expected?'

The Doctor was already reaching for his psychic paper but, as he did so, another person stepped into view from behind the butler. This was an old woman, with sharp, thin features and hard little eyes. Her gnarled hand grasped the top of an ornate walking stick.

'Doctor!' exclaimed the old lady. The dark eyes suddenly twinkled, and she seemed to shed twenty years in an instant. 'How good of you to come!'

'Umm...' began the Doctor, momentarily lost for words. 'Now, when I say we were expected... what I actually meant was...'

'Oh, never mind all that. You're here now and that's all that matters.' The old lady beamed at him, her eyes almost disappearing into a mass of wrinkles. She had a nice smile, but Gisella noticed that her teeth were very sharp and grey. 'You must excuse Stokes,' the old lady went on, indicating the imposing gentleman who had opened the door. 'He's a good butler but not what you'd call a "people-person". Move out of the way, Stokes, I can't see our new guests properly.'

The old lady slipped a pair of round, wire-framed spectacles onto her bony nose. The lenses were dark blue, like sunglasses. She peered carefully at the Doctor and then at Gisella. 'Oh! But you're not Doctor Black,' she exclaimed. 'And this certainly isn't Nurse White.'

'No,' agreed the Doctor. 'They... couldn't make it.'

'What an infernal nuisance! You must think I'm quite potty. Sorry, didn't catch your name...?'

'I didn't throw it,' beamed the Doctor. 'Doctor will do fine for me, anyway. And you are...?'

'Amelia Birch. Miss. Very pleased to meet you. And who's this charming young... girl?'

Gisella introduced herself with a small curtsey. It seemed appropriate, although the Doctor looked at her with some bemusement.

'You're absolutely delightful, my dear,' said Amelia Birch. She looked up at the Doctor. 'Is this your daughter?'

'No,' said the Doctor quickly. 'Definitely not my daughter. Someone else's daughter, actually.'

'Niece?'

'More a kind of ward,' the Doctor explained.

'Quite,' replied Miss Birch. She looked at Gisella again and then removed her strange glasses, smiling. 'You must be tired after your long journey, anyway. Why don't you come in and Stokes can rustle up something for you – can't you, Stokes?'

'I can't imagine anything giving me greater pleasure,' growled Stokes.

'Before we come in,' said the Doctor, 'I wonder if you could settle an argument?'

'Argument?'

'Yes. On our way here, Gisella told me that Devastation Hall is situated in Surrey. But I say it's in Kent. I'm sure it's close to the county border, but...'

'I see,' said Miss Birch. She looked at the Doctor with twinkling eyes. 'Well, I'm going to have to disappoint both of you. Devastation Hall is in neither of those counties. In fact, it's not in any of the Home Counties.'

The Doctor raised his eyebrows. 'Really?'

'Let me show you.' Amelia Birch walked down the steps and headed off across the gravel.

They followed Miss Birch through the gardens until they reached a small row of trees. She led them through a gap and stopped, gesturing at the view beyond. The Doctor and Gisella joined her.

And gasped.

They were standing on what appeared to be the edge of a cliff. The ground simply fell away beneath their feet – and beyond, stretching away into infinity, was nothing but darkness.

They could see stars and floating wreaths of distant nebulae, glittering against a deep, black background. The land they stood on – along with the house, the gardens and trees – was nothing more than a tiny island floating in space.

'I don't understand,' Gisella said in awe. She looked back through the trees at the house, lit by the evening sunlight, and then again at the view in front of her – nothing but stars. 'Where are we?'

'You've stepped beyond the environment bubble which surrounds my house and its grounds,' explained Miss Birch softly. 'Take another step and you will pass through the atmospheric field. And then you will find yourself in the cold, deadly vacuum of space.'

The Doctor gazed in consternation at the stars

around them. 'The Silver Devastation,' he whispered.

'It's not possible,' said Gisella, shaking her head.

The Doctor pulled her gently back from the abyss. 'Best not to go too near the edge,' he advised. 'It literally is the end of this world.'

'But I'm sure you didn't come all the way here to admire the scenery – or lack of it,' said Miss Birch, clapping her hands to signify that the tour was over. 'We really must be getting on. I do have other guests to attend, you know.'

'Really?' said the Doctor. 'Are we going to meet them?'

'But of course!'

Amelia Birch led them back through the trees towards the house. The sun was very low now – although Gisella failed to see how there could be any sun at all.

'Enclosed micro-climate,' muttered the Doctor, noticing her discomfort. 'Very useful if you want to survive on a tiny lump of rock floating in the middle of space. The sun is just a polarised energy field held in a containment sphere. It's closer than it looks too. Let's just hope nobody switches it off.'

'But this means that we are in the right place after all,' Gisella said quietly. 'The Darksmith Agent could be here.'

'Yes, that's true. Though I don't know how he thinks the Crystal can be destroyed in a place like this. But keep your eyes peeled. In the meantime, I want to find out what's going on...'

As they neared the house there was a sudden, bright flash in the sky. All three of them looked up, shielding their eyes against the glare of the fake sun, as a space ship roared overhead. It was small, sleek as a bullet and gleaming red.

'It's landing right in front of the house!' exclaimed Gisella.

'That's not allowed!' Miss Birch said disapprovingly. 'There is plenty of room for people to park their spaceships at the rear of the house.'

'Aw, the pilot just wants to show off,' the Doctor grinned as the rocket touched lightly down the gravel.

The engines died with a snarling flourish and the cockpit hatch slid open. A man jumped out and landed easily by the starboard engine. He was wearing spacer's boots, a long leather flying coat and a silk scarf. 'Hi there,' he called out. His black hair was slicked back from a handsome face and devilish grin. 'Horatio Hamilton,' he announced.

'Did I get here in time? I've been pushing this baby hard all the way from Altair 59. Made the trip in less than a day – didn't want to miss a thing.'

'Less than a day from Altair 59?' said the Doctor, sounding full of admiration. 'That's got to be a record. Well done.'

'Cheers,' said Horatio Hamilton, shaking the Doctor's hand enthusiastically. 'But I do have a reputation to keep.'

'Oh, you're *that* Horatio Hamilton,' realized the Doctor. 'Brilliant! You did the Mars-Centauri Grand Prix in under six parsecs – which is no mean feat, considering parsecs are measurements of space, not time. Bent the rules a bit, there, but never mind. It's the taking part that counts.'

'Which is why I'm here,' Hamilton grinned. He looked at Miss Birch. 'I am on time, aren't I?'

'Yes, of course,' the old lady said. 'You must come inside and meet the others. But first I'll have to ask you to move your spaceship. We can't leave it parked on the driveway like that, it spoils the view. There are full spaceport facilities to the rear of the house.'

'Got you,' Hamilton said, with a mock salute. He vaulted back into the cockpit of his rocket and started the engines. 'Go ahead, I'll catch you up.'

The ship rose slowly into the air and then shot off with a terrific roar. They watched Hamilton describe a perfect arc over the house and then disappear.

'What a fantastic spaceship,' Gisella said.

'Hmm,' agreed the Doctor. 'It must be to have got here all the way from Altair 59 since breakfast. Because it's not only a record – it's impossible.'

'We got here all the way from Earth in less time,' Gisella pointed out.

'Yes, but that was in the TARDIS. Different rules.'

'Come along, you two,' said Amelia Birch, herding them towards the house. 'Stop chattering and get inside. You've yet to meet the other guests, and Stokes is serving cocktails in the drawing room before all the killing begins.'

The Doctor stopped in his tracks. 'Killing?'

'Yes.'

'You know, that's the second time someone's mentioned killing since we arrived.'

'Oh dear. Sorry if we've spoiled it for you. But never mind – there's plenty more surprises to come that you know nothing about!'

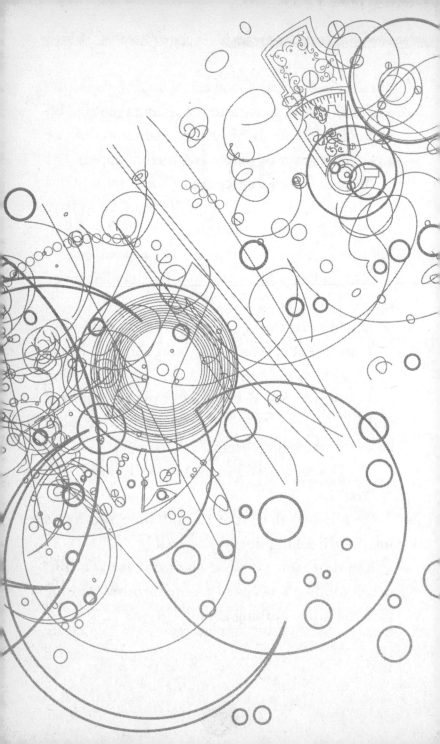

Cast List

Stokes was indeed serving cocktails in the drawing room.

'I'll have water, please,' said the Doctor. 'Shaken, not stirred.'

Stokes eyed him murderously and then sighed heavily. 'I'll see what I can do, sir.'

The Doctor grimaced. 'Tell you what, Stokes. I never did like all that servant stuff. Be a good lad and just call me Doctor.'

'Yes, sir. Whatever you say, sir.'

All the rooms in Devastation Hall were large and beautifully furnished. There were antiques dotted here and there, old masters adorned the walls, and the centrepiece of the drawing room was an enormous Adam fireplace complete with three thick logs in the grate. Fire crackled and snapped in the hearth, and there was a group of four people standing in the flickering glow.

They were all human – an older, bluff-looking gentleman with a military bearing dressed in tweeds; a slender, attractive woman in a red dress; a long-haired youth wearing earphones; and finally Miss Birch herself.

Stokes reappeared with a glass of water for the Doctor and a freshly squeezed orange juice for Gisella. 'Your drinks,' he intoned with barely any interest.

The Doctor sniffed his water and then sipped it, rolling the taste around his tongue like a connoisseur. 'Hmm. Excellent, Stokes. My compliments – you certainly know your water.' He took another sip and closed his eyes. 'Let me guess: melted ice water, running free in a mountain stream over – I'm guessing here – limestone rocks?'

Stoke raised an eyebrow. 'Straight from the tap, sir.'

'Oh. What about the lemon? Is that straight from the supermarket?'

'Twisted it myself, sir.' By the look in his eye, Stokes might have been referring to somebody's neck.

The Doctor smiled at him. 'Bottoms up, then.'

As Stokes moved away, Gisella stepped closer to the Doctor. 'Where did all this lot come from?' she asked in a low voice, nodding at the assembled guests.

'A board game by the looks of it,' muttered the Doctor. 'Remind me to have a look at that spaceport out the back later on. That should tell us quite a lot.'

'Good afternoon, everybody,' announced Amelia Birch loudly from the centre of the room. 'Or do I mean good evening? It is getting rather late, and I'm afraid that means we'll have to push on rather.'

There was a murmur of approval from the other guests.

'I suppose I should begin with the introductions,' Miss Birch continued. 'You all know me by now, of course. But, in no particular order, allow me to present each of you in turn...'

She raised a hand to indicate the military gentleman. 'This is General Augustus Korch...'

'Retired,' said the General.

'But none the worse for it as I'm sure you'll agree. General Korch fought in the last Dalek War. He was instrumental in securing the release of the infamous Aurora hostages – I'm sure you will all remember that particular incident, at least, those of us who are old enough! The news was positively full of it at the time.'

'It was all long ago,' said the General dismissively. 'No one wants to hear about that kind of thing nowadays.'

'But you're too modest, General! The General's come all the way from Sigmus Gamma IV to be with us this evening, and he really is most terribly welcome.'

Everyone raised their glasses to the General, who nodded and rumbled something back. He stood ramrod straight, as if he had never been able to leave the parade ground behind.

'Next is Miss Scarlett Plume,' announced their hostess. 'Although I'm sure she needs no introduction.'

Scarlett Plume – the beauty in the red dress – smiled dazzlingly. 'Hi, everyone – isn't this just the most exciting thing you've ever done?'

'Not quite,' murmured the Doctor into his water.

But Scarlett Plume heard him quite clearly. 'Oh, but it must be! Unless – don't tell me you don't know what you're here for yet?'

'Well... we came at the last minute, really.'

'Then you're in for a real surprise – and a treat.' Scarlett winked at the Doctor and raised her cocktail. 'Not to mention the most exciting time of your life.'

'We'll see,' smiled the Doctor. 'I've had quite a few exciting times in my lives.'

Miss Birch coughed politely. 'Moving on...' she said, 'Allow me to introduce Lenny Sprang.'

The young man with the earphones gave a bored wave, his Adam's apple bobbing up and down in his thin, white neck.

'Lenny won a trip here in a competition, didn't you, Lenny?'

'Yeah. Online hypernet competition. First place. I had to guess the exact galactic coordinates of Devastation Hall.'

'That's remarkable,' said the Doctor.

'I think you'll find that we're all remarkable here, Doctor,' said Miss Birch. 'Including yourself, of course. Everyone – this is the Doctor, with his young companion Gisella. I'm sure there's more to them than meets the eye, so watch out!'

There was a buzz of amusement and the Doctor and Gisella found themselves smiling self consciously.

'And I think that must be just about everyone,' Miss Birch said. 'Oh, no. Wait a minute. There's one or two missing...'

'Already?' spluttered General Korch. 'Don't tell me the killing's already started!'

'Yes, about the killing...' began the Doctor.

'All in good time,' said Miss Birch. 'You really must be patient, Doctor – otherwise there will be nothing to talk about at dinner.'

At that moment the door burst open and in swept Horatio Hamilton, still in his flying jacket and boots. 'Hi there, guys!' he called. 'Hope I'm not too late. Just left my ship out the back there – and look what I found on the way in, wandering around all lost.'

With him was an elderly man with a shock of frizzy grey hair and an extravagant beard. He was wearing a pair of old corduroy trousers and a baggy cardigan.

'Mr Hamilton, how good of you to join us at last. And you've found Professor Doofus! How marvellous.'

'Hello, everyone,' said Professor Doofus cheerily. 'Sorry I'm a bit late!'

'Oh you're not late *yet*, professor,' tittered Miss

Birch, and everyone tittered along with her.

Everyone except the Doctor and Gisella.

'Can anyone tell us,' Gisella said at last, 'what exactly we're all here for?'

'Why, my dear,' smiled Miss Birch indulgently. 'Isn't it obvious? We're here to play the Game of Death.'

The Game of Death

The Doctor straightened his bow tie and checked his reflection in the mirror. He'd worn this dinner suit before, and it never boded well.

'You look funny,' said Gisella, coming into the console room.

'Thanks,' the Doctor said. 'You look hilarious.'

Gisella looked down at the long evening dress she was wearing. She had found it in the TARDIS wardrobe room. The skirt was very full and if she took hold of a handful of material on either side she could pull it right out like a parachute. 'It was the only thing that fitted me.'

'It's perfect.'

'Well I feel like a right ninny. I don't see why we've got to dress up like this anyway.'

'Miss Birch said it was a formal dinner. That

means black tie. For me, anyway. You need a dress.'

'I kept my trainers on,' Gisella confessed, lifting the skirt up to show her running shoes. She had worn them on the advice of the Doctor when she first travelled in the TARDIS. There was a lot of running involved when you travelled with the Doctor.

'Me too,' the Doctor smiled, waggling a foot. He'd swapped his old canvas trainers for a clean pair in black and white, to match the dinner suit. He extended an arm. 'Shall we go?'

Outside, the sky was dark and there was a full moon looking down on them like a giant silver eye.

'How can there be a moon?' wondered Gisella. 'I thought this was an artificial climate.'

'It's not a moon,' said the Doctor, looking up as they walked. 'It's just the sun turned down. There's probably a control for it somewhere. I wonder if they use thermotronic excitation?'

'I think we've got more to worry about than that,' said Gisella. 'What do you think this Game of Death thing is all about?'

'I've no idea. But I think we're going to find out.'

'And don't forget the Darksmith Agent,' Gisella

warned, keeping her voice low. 'That thing could be anywhere here – waiting for us.'

The Doctor pulled a face. 'A dirty great metal and plastic robot? I think we'd spot it around here.'

As they walked through the gardens, Gisella drew closer to the Doctor. The moonlight – or whatever light it was – cast long black shadows around them. It wasn't hard to imagine that strange, unknown things were watching them closely from the darkness.

'I thought I heard something,' Gisella said suddenly. 'In the trees.'

'It's your imagination,' said the Doctor.

'No, seriously. My hearing is a lot better than yours. There's something moving in the trees, in the shadows... it's following us.'

Gisella's android hearing was undoubtedly superior, and the Doctor stopped to peer into the darkness. 'I can't see anything...'

Gisella pulled him along. 'Don't stop.'

'Hang on. You said you could hear something following us through the shadows. Aren't you even curious to know what it is?'

'Frankly, no. I'll be curious once we're in Devastation Hall.'

The Doctor allowed himself to be pulled along as they hurried through the night. There were no birds or animals here, nothing to make a sound except for their own footsteps. It was a strange and unreal journey, and it was difficult not to imagine any kind of danger lurking in the night.

Eventually they neared the hall in complete and eerie silence. Gisella clutched the Doctor's hand and whispered, 'At least we know it can't be the Agent following us.'

The Doctor wasn't convinced. 'That robot is extremely advanced. It could move like a jungle cat if it wants to. We wouldn't hear a thing.'

'That's not very reassuring.'

The Doctor put a finger to his lips, looking serious, and indicated a nearby hedge.

Gisella had, of course, heard it too – the sound of a low, coarse breathing from the other side. Cautiously they peered around the hedge.

'Hullo again!' said Ted, the gardener. He was closing a pair of heavy trap doors set into the ground by the wall and breathing heavily with the effort.

'Ted!' exclaimed the Doctor with relief.

The old man straightened up and regarded them both with a smile. 'Well, don't you two look a picture? All dressed up...'

'...and nowhere to go, yes.' The Doctor nodded at the trap doors. 'What's down there, then? Wine cellar?'

'Among other things, yes. The environmental controls for the asteroid are down there.'

'Really?' The Doctor stuck his hands in his pockets and looked up at the moon. 'So you look after all that as well as the gardens?'

'Everything, yes. My official title is Site Manager.'

'Which makes you the most important person here,' the Doctor grinned. 'After us. Well, good evening, Ted. Don't work too hard.'

Ted touched his cap. 'Evening to you, Doctor, Miss Gisella.'

'Will we see you tomorrow?' asked Gisella.

'I doubt that, miss. I doubt that very much indeed.'

'Why?'

'Well, the killing's due to start soon. Any moment, I'd say.'

'Of course!' exclaimed the Doctor as if he'd completely forgotten. 'The killing! Come on, Gisella. Hurry up, we don't want to miss all the killing, do we?'

She hurried after him, waving an uncertain goodbye at Ted. He waved back at them, looking rather sad.

At the hall, everyone was ready for dinner. They were all in evening dress, and the Doctor was secretly relieved. He'd turned up at parties before where he was the only person in a bow tie and it was always awkward.

'Doctor!' called out Miss Birch from the far side of the room. 'You're last to arrive – but you're not late yet!'

She laughed and the Doctor smiled dutifully as he accepted a glass of champagne. 'You've already used that joke,' he told her, 'and it wasn't very funny the first time.'

'Don't be such a party pooper,' she retorted. 'Let's go in for dinner.'

The dining room was dominated by a long mahogany table set for eight, and a series of ornate candelabras cast a flickering glow across the faces of the assembled guests. Stokes was serving soup with immaculate precision from a silver service.

'What's for pudding?' asked the Doctor. 'I hope it's Spotted Dick with custard.'

'That's for me to know,' said Stokes quietly, 'and you to find out.'

The Doctor turned to Gisella. 'Ooh, I love a mystery, don't you?'

'So,' began Miss Birch from her position at the head of the dining table. 'The Game of Death.'

A breathless hush fell over the room until Scarlett Plume asked, with breathless excitement, 'When does it start?'

'It already has,' replied Miss Birch, and she was rewarded with a collective gasp from around the table. 'It is a very simple game, based on one of life's universal goals: Survival.'

She allowed a cold silence to develop for a few seconds before adding, with a smile, 'And prize money worth a staggering one hundred million galactic credits, of course.'

There was much excitement over this, but Gisella noticed that the Doctor remained utterly unmoved. He had fixed Miss Birch with an unwavering, steely glare. 'What is it that we have to survive?' he asked.

The room quietened immediately. 'Somewhere on this asteroid is a living Nocturn,' Miss Birch said quietly. 'A creature renowned throughout the galaxy as a vicious, merciless predator. It hunts, it kills. That is all you need to know about the Nocturn.'

'Not quite,' said the Doctor. He looked more grim than Gisella had seen him before. 'There's more to it than that.'

Horatio Hamilton had loosened his collar. 'You heard what she said: it hunts, it kills – and it's somewhere on this asteroid. Isn't that enough?'

'Can't you give us a clue as to where the thing is?' asked General Korch.

'It could be anywhere,' said the Doctor. Such was the authority in his voice that everyone turned to listen. 'And I mean that literally. It could even be in this room with us, right now.'

'What? Don't tell me it's invisible!'

'Disguised. A Nocturn will grow an outer shell which exactly mimics the life forms it hunts – such as human beings. The likeness is precise in every detail. It could be any one of us.'

'Preposterous!' exclaimed General Korch.

'No,' said Miss Birch. 'The Doctor is perfectly correct. The Nocturn is a natural master of disguise, and it could – in theory – be posing as a guest here.'

'Ridiculous!'

'It's not even fair!'

There was a clamour of protest until the Doctor abruptly stood up and roared for quiet. 'We're all in this together,' he said in the silence that followed. 'And it shows, when we stand, hand in hand... oh, sorry, that's *High School Musical*. What I mean is – let's not panic...'

'At least not immediately,' said Gisella quietly.

'Not helping, Gisella.' The Doctor turned back to their host. 'Miss Birch, this is not a game – it's just an insane opportunity for murder and mayhem. Nocturns don't play by any kind of rules. We will be lucky if any one of us survives the night...'

'That's why the prize money is so high, Doctor. And the Nocturn does adhere to one important rule: it can only hunt at night time.'

'It *is* night time,' said Lenny Sprang.

'But surely we would know if one of us was an alien imposter,' argued Professor Doofus. 'We could find out soon enough through a system of simple checks.'

'I'm ahead of you, professor,' said the Doctor, producing his sonic screwdriver. 'A quick biometric scan should show if any of us are hiding something.'

And in that instant every single candle extinguished and the room was plunged into total darkness.

And then the screaming began.

Run!

There was instant chaos.

Everyone was shouting at once, and somebody was crying. There was the sound of breaking glass as something was knocked over in the dark. People were trying to stand, reaching out blindly in confusion and panic. Voices rose stridently in the blackness:

'It's in here!'

'Someone find the light switch!'

'Why's it so dark?'

'Is it in here? Is the monster in here now?'

Gisella couldn't see a thing, but she felt someone grab her by the hand. The Doctor! He started pulling her through the darkness, bumping into chairs and people all the way.

She heard a door slam and then the Doctor's long face sprang into view, lit by a bicycle torch he had somehow produced from his tuxedo pocket.

'What's happening?' Gisella asked.

'Shh,' he said, finger to his lips. 'We're in the hall.'

'What's happened to the lights? Is it because of the Nocturn? Miss Birch said it can only hunt at night...'

The Doctor shook his head. 'It can hunt anywhere, anytime, but it's extremely sensitive to light. That's why the game will take place overnight.'

'It's not much of a game.'

'I know. Stay here a moment, while I see what's going on.' And with that he ducked back through the doorway leading to the dining room.

Gisella followed him inside, stealing herself in case they stumbled on a live Nocturn chewing its way through the rest of the guests. The Doctor's torch roved quickly around the room, across the table, still covered with plates and dishes, and then a number of overturned chairs.

But there was no one else in there.

'They've scattered,' the Doctor said, sounding disappointed. 'They shouldn't have scattered. Scattering is the last thing they should have done. We should have all stayed together.'

'Surely it would be best if we split up?'

'And give the Nocturn a chance to pick us off one by one? That's exactly what it wants.'

'So why did you drag me out into the hall then?'

'Because I don't want to play this game, Gisella. We have other things to think about, remember: the Darksmiths, the Eternity Crystal, not to mention a homicidal robot.' The Doctor picked up a candelabra and found a box of matches. Quickly he lit the candles and gave the candelabra to Gisella. 'Here, hold this.'

'Where are we going now?' she asked as he headed for the exit. Typically he didn't even reply, and she was left with no choice but to follow. The flames flickered as she moved, casting eerie shadows across the walls. The Doctor led her through the darkened corridors to the rear of the house.

Suddenly there was a blood-chilling scream and Gisella almost dropped the candelabra in shock. The Doctor darted forwards, heading for the commotion. There was a horrible, tearing sound and a strangulated cry. Gisella followed him around the corner and they both stopped in their tracks. Lying on the floor was a body.

'It's Lenny,' said the Doctor, kneeling down. 'He's dead.'

Music played tinnily through the dropped earphones. 'Did... did the Nocturn do that to him?'

'I should think so.'

Gisella held the light closer to the body. Lenny Sprang's face was completely white, his cheeks sunken and his lips almost blue. 'He – he looks so pale.'

'The Nocturn paralyses its prey and then drains the blood out of it,' explained the Doctor stonily. 'Every last drop.'

'That's horrible. Awful.'

The Doctor switched off the music. Then he stood up and took Gisella gently by the arm. 'Come on, let's keep moving. There's nothing more we can do for him now, I'm afraid.'

Gisella followed him to a large door that led outside. It was locked, but a moment's work with the sonic screwdriver soon had it open. The cool night air greeted them as they stepped into the moonlight.

There was a wide balcony behind the house which overlooked the gardens at the rear. Leaning on the balustrade was Scarlett Plume.

'Don't take another step!' Scarlett said hurriedly. 'Look at the ground!'

The Doctor and Gisella looked down. The patio was made from a series of regular hexagonal paving stones. It looked innocent enough, but there was a definite note of warning in Miss Plume's voice.

'What wrong with it?' asked Gisella.

'Remember that we're all playing the Game of Death,' said Miss Plume. 'The patio activated after I walked across it...'

'Activated?' The Doctor fished out a coin and then tossed it experimentally onto the paving stones. The coin promptly vanished with a sharp sizzle. 'Ouch. Better watch our step.'

Gisella was appalled. 'We can't cross that!'

'All we need is a safe route across. There must be a clue.' The Doctor produced his sonic screwdriver and waved it across the patio. In the blue light a single random letter materialised on each flagstone. 'There we are – each stone is inscribed with a letter in ultraviolet. The answer's pretty obvious when you think about it! Now follow my footsteps – exactly!'

The Doctor stepped carefully across the hexagonal stones, taking a very particular route. Gisella followed and soon they were standing next to Miss Plume.

'How did you know which stones were safe?' asked Scarlett.

'I just looked for the correct path,' said the Doctor.

Activity

There is one safe route through the flagstones. Can you find the correct path?

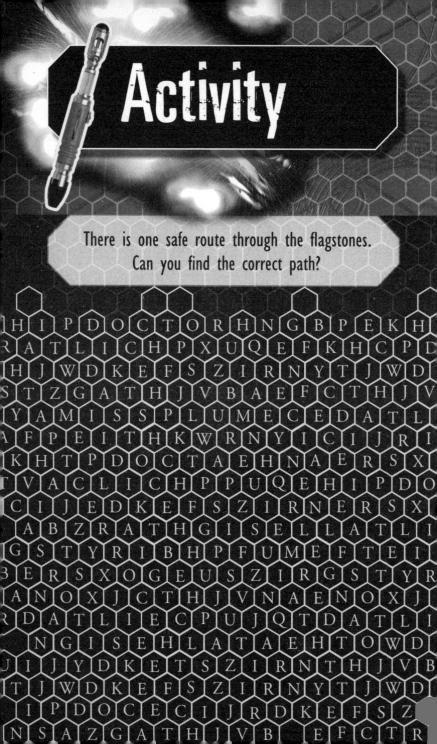

'Thank goodness you're here, anyway. Did you hear that dreadful scream?'

'Yes, it was Lenny Sprang. He's dead – killed by the Nocturn.'

'Oh my gosh.' Scarlett Plume ran a hand back through her long hair and swallowed. 'I didn't really believe... When the lights went out I just ran. I came out here for some air. But this is terrible...'

'Doctor,' said Gisella warily. 'If the Nocturn can disguise itself as one of the guests...'

'Then it could be Miss Plume,' agreed the Doctor.

Miss Plume looked shocked. 'You think I'm the monster? Oh, don't be ridiculous! Do I look like a monster to you?'

'It can disguise itself!' argued Gisella. 'It could be anybody!'

'Then it could just as easily be one of you two!'

'Except it isn't.'

'I only have your word for that, dear.'

'Likewise.'

'Look, we can go around in circles like this all night,' interrupted the Doctor. He turned to Gisella. 'And in all likelihood, if Miss Plume really was the Nocturn, we'd be dead by now.'

'I still think we should make sure,' Gisella insisted. 'Scan her.'

'Scan me all you like,' Miss Plume said.

The Doctor produced his sonic screwdriver. And at that same instant, another shrill scream tore through the night air.

'Oh no! Not another one!'

'It came from the gardens!' yelled the Doctor, setting off at a run.

Gisella hurried after him, pausing only to give the candelabra to Scarlett Plume. The lawns sloped down to another paved area flanked by steps. There were garden statues dotted all around, looming out of the night like ghosts as they passed.

The Doctor stopped suddenly, crouching down to examine something in the shadow of a large statue. When Gisella caught up she gave a little gasp of sorrow. General Korch was lying on the grass, staring lifelessly up at the moon.

Gently the Doctor closed the old man's eyes. 'He fought for his planet, risking his life for millions – and then died for a game,' he said bitterly. 'That's two lives lost in as many minutes.'

Gisella shuddered. It suddenly felt very cold. 'The Nocturn must be out here somewhere.'

'This way,' said the Doctor.

At the bottom of the garden a bright light suddenly flared and a number of large, metallic shapes were thrown into view. The arrival of the Doctor and Gisella had obviously triggered some security lights, because they had reached the edge of the spaceport. There were various craft, each sitting in its own landing bay.

'All the starships belonging to the guests,' said the Doctor.

'Something's moving over there,' said Gisella pointing at the nearest bay, where a sleek red ship stood upright and ready for blast off.

'That's Horatio Hamilton's ship,' said the Doctor.

As they approached the rocket, they found Hamilton busy plugging a thick power hose into a hatch on the side of the ship. The cable led back to a heavy piece of machinery at the side of the landing bay.

Hamilton hurried across to the power machine and activated it. A loud hum filled the air and pulses of light shot along the cable and into his ship.

'Getting ready for take-off?' asked the Doctor casually, hands in pockets.

Hamilton looked up, startled. 'Don't creep up on me like that! I nearly had a heart attack!'

'You're refuelling your ship,' observed Gisella. 'You're going to make a run for it, aren't you?'

'I'm not staying here a second longer than I have

to,' Hamilton admitted. 'It's absolute madness. I'm not hanging around here to be killed.'

'I thought that was the point,' said the Doctor. 'Don't you want the prize money?'

'I'm a successful racing pilot,' said Hamilton. 'I'm already rich.'

'Then why did you want to take part in the Game of Death?'

'I thought it was the celebrity version, if you must know. The one they do for charity – where the contestants are only stunned.'

'The Game of Unconsciousness?' suggested the Doctor.

'Laugh if you want to, Doctor. But I'm no fool. As soon as this thing's fuelled up I'm getting out of here. And if you two had any sense, you'd go too.'

'And leave everyone here to die?' the Doctor pulled a face. 'Nah – not my style. And hopefully not yours, either...'

'What do you mean?'

'No one could make it all the way here from Altair 59 in less than a day, not even in a ship like this.' The Doctor rapped the red hull with a knuckle. 'I dunno why you lied about that, but I think you're still lying now. You've got no intention of leaving just yet. Not until you've got what you want, anyway.'

'The prize money?' wondered Gisella.

Hamilton stared at them. 'Forget the prize money. The Nocturn is just a killing machine.'

'Yes, we know. It's already killed Lenny Sprang and General Korch.'

'That's... very unfortunate.' Hamilton ground his teeth together. Then he adjusted a control on the fuelling machine, turning the power dial up to full to speed up the recharge. 'But I'm not going to be the next victim.'

The spaceport lights suddenly faded, leaving the three of them in semi-darkness. The only light now came from the pulsating power hose connected to Hamilton's space ship.

Instinctively the three of them drew closer to the glow as the shadows gathered around them.

'What's going on?' asked Hamilton.

'It's the Nocturn,' said the Doctor.

'It's found us,' moaned Gisella. 'It must have been attracted by the lights.'

'It hunts in the shadows,' said the Doctor. 'Attacks when it's dark. It must be close by.'

'I'm scared,' whispered Gisella.

Then they all heard the low, throaty growl from the edge of the surrounding darkness.

Fight Back

It moved with a moist, sucking noise. Long, bony legs crept slowly forwards out of the shadows. Gisella wanted to hide her face, but she couldn't bear not to look – couldn't bear not to see what it was.

There were no visible details. Even in the light of the moon, she couldn't quite see the shape of it – nothing more than a hint of something large and as black as night. Something at the front glinted, jaws or pincers perhaps, coated in saliva.

She tried to hold the Doctor tighter, but then suddenly realized he wasn't there any longer. As the Nocturn surged forward with a horrible noise, the Doctor had dived to one side, rolling across the ground until he came up against the side of Hamilton's ship. He reached up, twisted the power hose out of its socket and then turned the nozzle towards the monster.

A brilliant light flared from the end of the cable. Gisella and Hamilton snapped their eyes shut and turned away as the Nocturn shrieked. It scuttled quickly backwards, away from the glare, and disappeared into the night.

The hum of the fuel station died as the Doctor switched it off. Darkness enveloped them once again. He dropped the cable and put his arms around Gisella. 'It's all right, it's gone now.'

'What did you do?' asked Hamilton, aghast.

'The Nocturn is very sensitive to light. I managed to unhook the power cable and drove it away with the energy surge.'

'Did you kill the thing?'

'I doubt it. The power cut out automatically, seconds after I disconnected the cable. But it's gone for now.'

Hamilton checked the power station. 'You stopped the refuelling process before it was complete. The energy banks won't be properly charged. I'll have to start again!'

'Don't be so ungrateful,' said Gisella. 'The Doctor just saved your life.'

The pilot hesitated. 'I'm sorry. You're right. If there's anything I can do... Look, there's only room for two in my ship. I can take one of you with me, but not both. It's the best I can do.'

'No thanks,' Gisella said. 'We're staying together.'

The Doctor helped Hamilton fix the power hose in place again and activated the fuelling station. 'It'll take a while to fill up,' he said, 'but stand by. If worst comes to worst...'

Hamilton looked the Doctor in the eye. 'I understand. I'll take Gisella with me if you wish.'

'Thank you.'

'No way!' Gisella protested. 'I'm with you!'

'Gisella, I've got to find that Nocturn and stop it – permanently. Otherwise everyone here will die. But if anything goes wrong... you've got to think of the Eternity Crystal.'

'If anything does go wrong then I'll be right there with you.'

'Good, because I'll need some help. But I want to know that Hamilton will be here for you, just in case.'

Hamilton nodded. 'I will.'

Gisella bit her lip. 'All right. Do you have a plan?'

The Doctor grinned. 'Of course I have a plan!'

They headed back to the house. It looked dark and forbidding, silhouetted against the night sky. A grey mist was seeping around the edges.

'At least we know who isn't the Nocturn,' said Gisella. 'It can't be Scarlett Plume, because she was on the terrace when we heard the second scream. And it isn't Horatio Hamilton, because he was with us when the Nocturn attacked.'

'And we can rule out Lenny Sprang and General Korch.'

'Which only leaves Miss Birch, Stokes the butler, Professor Doofus and Ted the Site Manager.'

'Still quite a list of suspects,' mused the Doctor. 'Although you've missed one out.'

'Who?'

'Me.'

'But it can't be you.'

'Why not? We were all in the dark when the lights went off in the dining room. Who's to say that the Nocturn didn't disguise its outer shell as me, grab your hand and pull you out?'

'You're kidding,' Gisella said. 'I'd know. And I was with you when the others were killed – and when the Nocturn attacked us on the landing bay.

You're just trying to scare me.'

'I'm trying to make you think. The Nocturn won't hesitate to kill either of us, and it will show no mercy. We have to be prepared.'

'So what's the plan?'

'First things first – we need to get the lights back on.' They had reached the house. The Doctor led her around the side until they reached the doors set into the ground by the wall. He opened them with his sonic screwdriver and then went down the steps into the cellar.

It was pitch black and smelled of damp. The Doctor fished out his bicycle lamp and shone it around. There were some old tables, a number of dusty wine racks and, in the corner, a large control panel.

'Here we are,' said the Doctor. He handed the torch to Gisella and then, putting on his glasses, quickly checked the controls over. 'It all seems to be in order. Someone must have rigged it to switch off automatically during dinner.'

'Can we switch the lights back on from here?'

'Oh yes.' The Doctor brandished his sonic screwdriver. 'It's just a question of finding the right control frequency.'

Activity

CORRECT FREQUENCY!
ACTIVATE LIGHT SYSTEM!

Which sonic frequency is the correct one?

SONIC FREQUENCY 1

SONIC FREQUENCY 2

SONIC FREQUENCY 3

SONIC FREQUENCY 4

'Ha! Easy! It's setting number two.' The Doctor ran the sonic screwdriver over the control panel and it hummed into life, indicator lights flashing on, power readouts glowing. Gradually, the generator came back on line and the cellar lights started to come on.

'Good evening,' said Stokes.

Gisella jumped as the butler stepped into the light. His face looked as grave as ever, his eyes hooded.

'Hello!' replied the Doctor cheerfully. 'Just thought I'd pop down and mend the lights. Must've been a fuse or something!'

'No,' said Stokes, 'it was a deliberate attempt to plunge us all into darkness and thereby leave us at the mercy of the Nocturn.'

'Ah well, I can't be right all the time.'

'At least the lights are back on, anyway,' said Gisella.

'It won't stop the Nocturn, miss,' said Stokes gloomily. 'It can move around all day, concealed beneath a protective carapace evolved to emulate its prey. Unsuspected, it will move closer... and closer...' Stokes stepped slowly towards Gisella as he spoke. 'Until it is standing right next to them.

Then, under the cover of darkness, it will emerge from beneath its shell and strike.' His eyes widened suddenly and Gisella gulped.

'You're scaring my friend,' said the Doctor. 'Stop it.'

'Fear is nature's way of protecting us,' Stokes replied. 'I'm just giving it a helping hand.'

'Yes, well don't. Come over here and tell me about this instead.' The Doctor nodded at the computer panel. 'This controls the climate for the asteroid, doesn't it? The atmosphere bubble and all that?'

'I believe it does.'

The Doctor tried some of the controls experimentally, stabbing buttons and twisting dials.

'I wouldn't try that, sir,' said Stokes. 'You might accidentally switch off the atmosphere bubble which surrounds the house and kill us all.'

The Doctor clicked his tongue. 'Oh, I doubt that. These controls are security coded.'

'They are the responsibility of the Site Manager.'

'You mean old Ted,' nodded the Doctor. 'So, only he knows the correct access code. Without that, it doesn't matter what I do. The controls won't function for me.'

'That is the general idea, yes.'

The Doctor aimed his sonic screwdriver at the computer panel but nothing happened. He made a few adjustments and tried again, but with the same result. 'Deadlocked,' he announced unhappily.

Stokes frowned. 'That shouldn't be possible.'

'And yet...' the Doctor spun the screwdriver, caught it and slipped it back into a pocket. 'It is.'

'Which means what?' asked Gisella.

'Which means I can't access the environment controls without Ted.'

'Why would you want to?'

'If I can change the power radiance setting from moon to sun – in other words, switch the night off and turn the day back on – then we might stand a chance against the Nocturn.'

'But you need Ted.'

'Yes.'

A distant scream echoed through the cold cellar.

'The Nocturn,' gasped Gisella.

'It's struck again,' Stokes realized.

The Doctor was already heading for the exit. He bounded up the steps and Gisella followed him out with Stokes.

On the gravel, not far from the cellar doors,

was another body. The pallid, unshaven features were withered and almost unrecognisable. But there was no mistaking the flat cap and the wheelbarrow nearby.

'It's Ted!' said Gisella.

'Dead,' added Stokes.

The Doctor straightened up, grim-faced. 'And without him, it's going to stay night time. Permanently.'

Closing In

'There must be a back-up code somewhere,' said Gisella. She was trying to think, but it was difficult with a corpse lying at her feet. It made her feel very strange.

The Doctor leapt to his feet. 'That's it! Back-up code. Plan B! Brilliant!' He grabbed her hand and pulled her after him. They skidded around the side of the house and ran up to the front door. The Doctor raced up the steps and yanked the bell pull.

They stood and waited, the Doctor bouncing from foot to foot with anticipation. 'Come on, come on... answer the door!'

The front door was opened a minute later by Miss Birch. The Doctor slipped past her, pulling Gisella with him, before she had a chance to object.

'Miss Birch,' the Doctor began, 'I've got some bad news. The Nocturn has already struck. It's killed Lenny and the General, and now Ted...'

'Ted's dead?'

'Yes. Ted's dead.'

'The Game of Death continues,' Miss Birch intoned.

The Doctor raised a finger. 'Precisely. We've got to stop it.'

'You can't stop it.'

'Yes I can. But I need the security code for the atmospheric environment controls in the basement.'

'And only Ted knew it,' Gisella explained.

'And Ted's dead.'

'And what,' Miss Birch said in a cold, brittle voice, 'do you think I can do about that? This is the Game of Death. Whether you like it or not, Doctor, people will die.'

'That's a rather cold-blooded attitude,' said the Doctor.

'Perhaps. But everyone dies eventually. Why not die trying to win a fortune?'

'That idea is wrong in so many ways,' the Doctor said, 'that I simply haven't got time to list them.'

'I'm so glad.'

Miss Birch walked calmly past them and into the living room. With a growl of impatience the Doctor darted after her. 'Miss Birch, I can stop the Nocturn. All I need to do is turn night into day. Now that would be a tall order even for me, in normal circumstances, but this asteroid is surrounded by an artificial environment bubble. I can switch the sun and moon around like *that*.' The Doctor clicked his fingers loudly. 'All I need is the security code to override the deadlock on the environment controls.'

Miss Birch frowned. 'Deadlock?'

'Somewhere on this asteroid there will be back-up data for the security code,' insisted the Doctor urgently. 'Can you tell me where to find it?'

Miss Birch thought for a moment. 'Of course.'

'Brilliant!'

'But I'm not going to.'

'Not brilliant.'

Gisella stepped forward. 'Miss Birch, you have to tell us!'

'Actually,' said the Doctor, 'I don't think she wants to, Gisella.'

Miss Birch was smiling at them both. She looked at Gisella and said, 'If I were you, dear, I would run. Run *now*, and run fast.'

'What do you mean?'

'There's more to you than meets the eye,' Miss Birch told her. 'I saw that the moment I met you.' She held up the pair of blue-tinted spectacles. 'These allow me to see beyond the normal human spectrum. Whatever you may be, I'm not interested in you. So run. Start running now. And don't stop.'

Gisella backed away. She didn't like the way Miss Birch was smiling at her, an evil, cruel smile that revealed rows of tiny grey teeth as sharp as needles.

'Do as she says,' said the Doctor. 'You know where to go.'

Gisella looked at him. 'But why? And what about you?'

'I was right when I said she was cold-blooded,' the Doctor said, nodding towards Miss Birch. 'But I didn't realize how right.'

Before Gisella could move or say anything else, Miss Birch began to change. It was an ugly, unnatural transformation. Her whole body seemed to split in two, starting from the head. With a terrible, moist rasp the two halves folded back like wings, revealing a mass of waving legs like the underside of a centipede.

Its head, projecting on a long, articulated stalk, held a cluster of unblinking, red eyes and a curving jaw full of serrated fangs.

'The Nocturn,' gasped Gisella. 'It was Miss Birch all along!'

The Doctor grabbed Gisella by the waist and propelled her towards the door. 'Run! Go to the spaceport!'

Gisella twisted around, about to ask what he thought he was going to do, only to find the door slamming in her face. With the Doctor on the other side of it.

The Doctor let go of the door handle and flung himself to the floor as the Nocturn attacked. Its powerful mandibles tore splinters out of the woodwork, raking down towards him for the death blow.

He rolled, once, twice, and then crawled underneath the coffee table. The Nocturn landed on top of it with a savage roar, and the furniture cracked beneath its weight.

The Doctor scrambled out, narrowly avoided another slash from the jaws, and hauled himself over the nearest settee. It tipped over, crashing on top of him as the monster shredded the upholstery. The Doctor crawled away, pulling himself up behind the floor-length curtains which hid the window. Quickly he climbed onto the broad windowsill. It was dark outside, and his reflection stared back at him worriedly.

Suddenly the curtains were ripped away, the Nocturn thrashing its head from side to side to free its jaws of the velvet drapes. The Doctor hurriedly fiddled with the window latch as he turned to look at the creature.

'You're not the woman you used to be, Miss Birch!' he said.

The empty shell that formed Miss Birch flapped like dragonfly wings on the Nocturn's back. Its crimson eyes bulged as they regarded the Doctor with deadly intent. The window latch was stuck fast. He was trapped and the monster knew it.

Its long, lethal proboscis began to emerge from between its jaws with an eager thirst.

The Doctor jumped up, grabbed the curtain rail above the window and swung himself at the Nocturn. His feet collided with the creature's head, knocking it backwards. It screamed with outrage. The Doctor twisted around, altering his grip on the curtain pole like a gymnast on the parallel bars, and let himself swing back towards the window. It smashed into a thousand pieces and then he hit the ground outside, rolling, back up on his feet more by luck than design. Shards of broken glass tumbled off his dinner suit as he sprinted away into the night.

Gisella ran as fast as she could – at least, she did once she had torn enough material off her ball gown. She had never doubted the Doctor, but this was the most difficult thing she had ever done. She wanted to go back and help, but she knew it would be futile. The Doctor wouldn't have thanked her for that. He would need all his concentration to outwit the Nocturn, and if she had stayed the distraction could have proven fatal.

She ran down the lawns at the back of the hall towards the spaceport. The lights were on and she could see Horatio Hamilton's rocket standing tall and ready to go. Gisella had no intention of leaving the Doctor, but perhaps she could persuade the pilot to help.

'Gisella!'

She turned and slowed as she heard her name

called. Scarlett Plume was running up behind her, one hand trying to raise the hem of her dress. In her other hand she held her red high heels.

'Wait for me!'

Gisella stopped. 'I'm not leaving,' she said. 'I've got to get help. The Doctor's in there with Miss Birch – she's the Nocturn!'

Scarlett frowned. 'Miss Birch?'

'She's already killed Lenny and the General – and Ted as well.'

'Ted's dead?'

'Yes!'

'So where are you going now?'

'Mr Hamilton is waiting to leave in his spaceship. Maybe he can help.'

'I doubt it,' said Scarlett. 'It looks like he's getting ready to blast off.'

Gisella turned. The rocket engines were indeed beginning to glow and she could already hear the motors whirring.

'Stop!' she screamed, running towards the landing bay. 'Stop!'

Scarlett Plume ran after her, shoes in one hand, bare feet pattering across the concrete apron. 'Stop! Mr Hamilton, stop!'

Hamilton was halfway up the short ladder which led to the cockpit. He turned when he heard their voices over the growl of the rocket engines.

'Wait! The Doctor told you to wait!' yelled Gisella accusingly.

'I'm just warming the engines up,' Hamilton said. He yanked off his helmet and flying goggles. 'Honest!'

'Never mind that,' Gisella shouted. 'The Doctor's in danger. He needs help!'

Reluctantly, Hamilton descended the ladder and walked across the landing bay towards her, pulling off his gloves. 'What can I do?'

'There's nothing you can do,' said Scarlett Plume.

Horatio Hamilton smiled at her, a rakish twinkle in his eyes. 'Don't be so sure, babe. I'm not your ordinary coward and cheat. There's more to me than you think.'

'And me,' said Scarlett.

With a horrible cracking sound, her body split open to reveal the Nocturn beneath.

Knock, Knock, Turn

The Doctor had been running for some way before he finally decided on where he should be running to. He altered course suddenly, his trainers skidding on the grass, and headed back towards the hall. He was pretty confident Miss Birch – or rather the Nocturn – wouldn't expect that. He hadn't expected it himself, after all, so how could she?

The lights were all on in the house now. He headed for one of the windows at the side of the house, away from the cellar. No point in going back there yet.

The window was locked from the inside. He used the sonic screwdriver to crack a pane of glass, tapped it free with his elbow and then carefully reached inside to free the latch. In a minute he was standing inside the kitchen.

He looked around for something useful. A rolling pin? Too primitive. Carving knife? Too sharp. Frying pan? Too comical.

'Spotted Dick and custard, sir?'

The Doctor whirled and came face to face with Stokes. He was holding a silver tray covered by a tureen. 'You're always popping up in unexpected places,' said the Doctor.

'On the contrary, sir,' replied Stokes solemnly. 'I am only ever where I expect to be.'

'Yes, I expect so.'

'It appears that the Mistress has taken a turn for the worse,' Stokes said.

'Ah, you noticed...?'

'If there is anything I can do to help?'

The Doctor thought for a moment and then suddenly exploded into life. 'Wait a minute! Did you say Spotted Dick?'

'I believe I did, sir.' Stokes held up the tray.

The Doctor removed the lid and a wisp of steam curled up from a large suet pudding dotted with currants and sultanas.

He looked up at the butler. 'And custard?'

The Nocturn drooled saliva from its clacking

mandibles. The pungent ooze sizzled where it hit the concrete. Gisella and Hamilton, their backs against the landing fins of the pilot's space ship, watched as the creature moved slowly towards them. Miss Scarlett's body flapped like wings behind its curved spine.

'But I saw Miss Birch *change*...' gasped Gisella. 'She was the Nocturn!'

'And so is Miss Scarlett,' said Hamilton regretfully.

'They never said there was going to be more than one!'

'It's a fix all right,' Hamilton nodded. 'The whole game – it's just as we suspected: nothing more than an elaborate front for a nest of killers. Well, it's time it was stopped.'

Hamilton took a plastic wallet from the leg pocket on his overalls and flipped it open. 'Commander Karl Zalenby,' he said to the approaching creature. His voice sounded suddenly cool and authoritative. 'Galactic Police. You're nicked.'

Gisella gaped. 'You're a policeman?'

He nodded. 'Undercover, posing as Horatio Hamilton. We've been after this lot for months.' He held the ID out towards the Nocturn as it approached. But with a vicious swipe of its forelegs, the ID wallet was dashed from Zalenby's hand.

'All right,' said Zalenby. 'If you want to play rough...' He reached into another pouch and produced a stubby laser pistol.

The Nocturn regarded the weapon curiously through its many red eyes.

'Take another step and I shoot,' said Zalenby. 'That's fair warning.'

The Nocturn halted, its jaws opening and closing as if in contemplation.

Without taking his eyes off the monster, Zalenby said to Gisella, 'I've been sent to investigate the Game of Death. We've been receiving a large number of complaints from bereaved next of kin.'

'I'm not surprised,' said Gisella.

'I've seen enough to know that it needs shutting down,' Zalenby continued. He raised his gun and aimed it squarely at the Nocturn. 'You're under arrest, madam.'

The Nocturn launched itself at Zalenby's throat, slamming him against the side of the rocket ship with a loud clang. The policeman slumped to the floor, unconscious, his laser pistol falling from his fingers.

With a hideous, gurgling roar of triumph,

the Nocturn bent over the man's body and a long, thin proboscis emerged from between its dripping mandibles.

The Doctor opened the kitchen door a crack and peered out. What he could see of the corridor outside was empty.

'Coast's clear,' he whispered. 'Let's go.'

Stokes followed him out. The Doctor started off in one direction, but the butler quickly called him back. 'This way, sir.'

'Are you sure?'

'I have one or two secrets myself,' Stokes replied. 'Including a secret route to the library at the rear of the house.'

Activity

Can you find the secret route from the kitchen to the library...without meeting the Nocturn?

Kitchen

Library

'Everyone seems to have secrets around here,' muttered the Doctor. 'I feel like I'm the only one with nothing to hide.'

'Are you sure about that, sir?'

The Doctor frowned. 'What do you mean?'

'You're not the usual type we get here,' Stokes said.

'I'm not the usual type you get anywhere,' the Doctor replied.

'I don't doubt that. But then neither is your companion, Miss Gisella. She isn't like you, but then she isn't quite like anything else I've ever met.'

'She is unique.'

'She isn't human.'

'Does that matter?'

'She's isn't anything. At least, nothing I can explain. Nothing I can call alive.'

The Doctor glanced curiously at him. 'What makes you say that?'

'All guests are routinely scanned by Miss Birch on arrival. It was clear that your companion was... most unusual.'

'That's why Miss Birch told her to run,' realized the Doctor. 'The Nocturn wasn't interested in her. No blood.'

'Would you care to explain that comment, sir?'

'Gisella is an android,' the Doctor said. 'A very sophisticated machine built by a master of robotic engineering. She's as close to being "alive" as any machine could be.'

'That's fascinating.'

'As far as I'm concerned Gisella is a living, thinking person. It doesn't matter to me one jot that she happens to be made out of metal and plastic compounds.'

'You mean it's *not* what's inside that counts?'

The Doctor gave Stokes a black look. 'You know what I mean.'

'I think I do. In other words, Gisella is not like the *other* machine.'

The Doctor froze. 'What other machine?'

'The other machine that is here. Another "living" thing made from metal and plastic.'

The Doctor gripped Stokes arm. 'Tell me: what did this other machine look like?'

'Tall, powerful, humanoid. Its internal mechanisms are visible through a transparent outer layer.'

'Where exactly did you see it?'

'On a number of occasions, in and around the grounds. It has been here for some time, but it conceals itself.' Stokes paused. 'Do you know what it is, sir?'

'I've a pretty good idea, yes. It's an Agent. It works for the Darksmith Collective.'

Stokes could see that the Doctor looked troubled. 'But what is it doing here at Devastation Hall? It can't play the Game of Death.'

'Oh, it's not playing.'

'I assume from your tone, sir, that this Agent machine is not welcome.'

'I'm an idiot!' the Doctor exploded. He ran his fingers through his hair. 'How could I have been so stupid? I thought I was being clever, following the Agent from Earth. But it's been one step ahead all the time. It wasn't leading us where *we* wanted. It lured us here. While we're caught up in the Game of Death, the Agent only has to wait for the chance to strike.'

'With respect, sir, I don't know what you're blithering on about. But you have been here for quite a while now. This Agent has had plenty of time to strike.'

'Then why hasn't it?' The Doctor suddenly slapped himself on the side of his head. 'Of course! It knows I'm a threat. It won't attack while I'm protecting Gisella...!'

'Which, I feel I must point out, you are not doing at the moment. Sir.'

'What?' The Doctor's eyes suddenly widened in fearful realization. 'Gisella! She's on her own!'

Gisella grabbed hold of the Nocturn and tried to pull it away from Zalenby. 'Leave him alone! He's done nothing wrong!'

The Nocturn was immensely strong. It barely seemed to notice her. Gritting her teeth, Gisella found the edge of its carapace and dug her fingers in hard. She was rewarded with a loud snarl, and the monster turned its head away from Zalenby to bite at her with its jaws. Drops of spit sizzled against her skin as she struggled. The mandibles, each serrated like a steak knife, slashed and snapped.

On the floor, Zalenby started to groan.

'Hamilton!' shouted Gisella. 'Or Zalenby, whatever your name is! Get up! Help me!'

The Nocturn wrenched itself from side to side, shaking Gisella off. She hit the ground hard and rolled over, but before she could get to her feet the thing was practically on top of her. Enraged, the monster let out a terrifying, squealing roar and

Gisella saw straight down its glistening pink gullet. Organs moved inside its throat as the proboscis emerged once again, probing towards her.

Gisella backed away on her heels and elbows as the creature advanced.

Behind the Nocturn, Zalenby sat up groggily.

Gisella smiled grimly. She had succeeded. She had distracted the creature from its human prey; it would find her an entirely different prospect.

But then the smile faded from Gisella's lips. Something rose up behind the Nocturn, blocking out the light from the moon. Silhouetted in its silver glow, a giant humanoid shape towered above both the monster and Gisella.

Powerful gears and servomotors whirred beneath transparent plastic armour. A pair of electronic eyes glowed in a metallic skull-like head.

It was the Darksmith Agent. And it had come for her.

All Together Now...

The Doctor ran through Devastation Hall at breakneck speed, heading for the rear of the house. That would be the quickest route to the spaceport area.

Somewhere behind him, Stokes followed at a more stately pace.

The Doctor skidded to a halt outside the door to the library. From what he could remember, the library overlooked the veranda at the rear. But when he tried the door, it was locked.

'Who'd want to lock up a library?' he wondered aloud. A second's work with the sonic had the lock sprung and the door flung wide. He darted inside, heading for the French windows at the back of the room which led onto the veranda.

And skidded to a stop once again.

There was a foot poking out from behind one of the reading desks. Fearing the worst, the Doctor peered cautiously behind the desk.

'The body in the library, I presume,' he said.

The figure crouching behind the desk looked up, his lined face a mask of anxiety beneath a crown of wild grey hair.

'Come on out, Professor Doofus,' said the Doctor. He bent down to help him up. 'I bet you were rubbish at hide and seek when you were a kid.'

'I don't remember ever being a child,' said the professor wearily.

'Aw, that's a shame. Think of all the things you used to do – all the hiding and running and having fun.'

'I never did any of that.'

'You wouldn't last five minutes with me.' The Doctor patted him on the back. 'Still, you're alive and that's what counts.'

'I locked myself in here straight away,' said the professor, his voice quivering with fear. 'I keep hearing the screams but I daren't come out. I'm such a coward.'

The Doctor scratched his head. 'Y'know, it's hard to understand why anyone would want to play the Game of Death, but you really don't seem cut out for it, professor...'

The door opened and Stokes came in, as cool and calm as ever. 'Ah, there you are, sir. And Professor Doofus – still alive. How thrilling.'

'Do you know who the Nocturn is yet?' asked Doofus.

'It's Miss Birch,' answered the Doctor vaguely, as if it really wasn't important. 'You know, something isn't adding up here...'

Stokes coughed politely into his fist. 'Excuse me, sir, but weren't you racing to save your young robot companion?'

The Doctor was still frowning, rubbing his chin in deep thought. 'Yes, yes, I was...'

'Then may I suggest exiting through the French windows at pace, sir.'

'What? Yes!' Suddenly galvanised into action again, the Doctor leapt right over the reading desk and bounded for the patio doors.

He flung them wide and the three of them went out into the cold, crisp night.

The moon picked out a familiar shape standing by the balustrade.

'Doctor,' said Miss Birch with a ghastly smile. 'At last – together in the moonlight. How romantic...'

Then she split wide open, revealing the hideous, snarling monster within.

As the Nocturn bore down on her, Gisella saw the robot behind it move with blinding speed. One swipe of its metal arm threw the Nocturn aside.

The Agent stepped towards Gisella, perhaps thinking that the Nocturn was irrelevant, but the monster had other ideas. With a roar, it hurled itself at the robot, landing on its broad shoulders, gripping it between its multiple legs and biting down hard. The mandibles screeched across the metal and plastic armour, trying to get a grip.

The Agent reached up, grabbed the Nocturn, trying to tear it off. But the creature was strong and determined. It clamped its legs around the robot's torso, and gripping one of the metal arms in its jaws, began to twist it savagely from side to side. The Agent tried to fire its built-in weaponry, but the Nocturn had badly damaged its arm.

The Agent realized it had a fight on its hands. The Nocturn lifted the robot and slammed it down onto the concrete with a resounding crash.

Gisella had crawled over to where Karl Zalenby lay by the spaceship. She helped him to sit up, but he looked awful. 'What's going on?' he asked, his words slurred.

'Difficult to say,' Gisella replied, glancing at the ferocious battle taking place on the landing bay. 'It looks like a fight to the death. Whoever wins will probably then kill us.'

The policeman climbed to his feet with help from Gisella. 'Where did that robot come from?'

'It's a long story. Let's get out of here.' Gisella pulled him along, dodging a flailing Nocturn leg.

The Agent had grabbed the creature's head with one arm and began to force it back. The Nocturn screamed, wrenching itself from side to side in a frenzy until the robot's grip was broken. The metal hand came away clutching a large piece of chitin and the Nocturn howled.

The Agent landed two rapid, heavy blows and the Nocturn folded. The creature sagged on its many legs, almost kneeling in defeat before the robot.

'This matter is settled,' said the Agent, before calmly reaching out and tearing the Nocturn's head clean off.

The Nocturn gave a massive shudder and then keeled over. The Agent discarded the head and scanned the area for its prey. Photothermic vision sensors picked out the body heat trail of Gisella and Zalenby leading off from the landing bay, deeper into the spaceport.

Swiftly, implacably, the Agent followed them.

'Stop!' the Doctor shouted, holding out his hands.

The Nocturn glared at him through its many eyes and gurgled hungrily. 'You have played the Game of Death,' it rasped, 'and you have lost.'

'I think I ought to warn you,' said the Doctor, 'I'm a very bad loser.'

'But no less edible for it!'

'You may have a point there,' agreed the Doctor. 'But I've got to hand it to you, that was some disguise. How do you do it? I mean, those things on your back that look like Miss Birch – what are they? Vestigial wings, evolved into a pliable shell? A bit like a ladybird. I love ladybirds!' he turned to Professor Doofus. 'Have you ever seen a ladybird?'

'No,' said the professor.

'Didn't think so. No childhood, no memories. What have you got, professor? A secret?'

The Doctor was glaring at him now, and the professor met his stare quite easily.

'A big, fat, *nocturnal* secret?'

'You think you're very clever, don't you, Doctor?' Professor Doofus' face twisted into a sneer, and then twisted again, wildly this time, until it separated straight down the middle, followed by the rest of his body. It looked as though he was turning inside out with a disgusting, wet sucking noise as the Nocturn emerged.

Both Nocturns began to stalk towards the Doctor and Stokes.

'I had you worked out in the library, mate,' the Doctor said to the creature that had been Professor Doofus. 'I knew there had to be more than one Nocturn. There was no way Miss Birch here could have killed both Lenny and General Korch. It's a bit of a cheat, then, the Game of Death. Isn't it?'

'I'm afraid so, sir,' said Stokes.

'How many more of these things are there, Stokes?'

Stokes shrugged. 'Enough.'

'Enough for what?'

'Enough to ensure that there are never any survivors.'

Slowly the Doctor turned to look at the butler. There was something in his tone that wasn't quite right, even for Stokes. Something that made the hairs on the back of the Doctor's neck stand up.

'Oh, not you too,' he said.

Stokes loomed over him. The butler's head peeled away from the black carapace beneath, revealing bulbous red eyes and a slavering mouth between giant pincer-like jaws. His body folded back against the Nocturn's shoulders and the legs scrabbled free.

The Doctor was surrounded. Slowly, the trio of monsters closed in. The Doctor stood at the centre of the triangle, looking from one to the next, but there was no way out.

'I suppose you think you've got me exactly where you want me,' he said. 'But you'd be wrong. It's actually the other way around.'

He held up his sonic screwdriver. The Nocturns growled, unimpressed. They knew the sonic device couldn't harm them.

'I tried to fix the environment controls in the cellar so that false moon up there switched over to the sun. I was hoping you wouldn't be able to function so well in broad daylight. But for it to work properly, I really needed you all out in the open, like this. Disguised wouldn't work at all – you'd be just like the humans you imitated so well. I saw that when we arrived.'

The Nocturns, evidently listening, halted their

advance. They were close enough for the Doctor to be able to feel their fetid breath on his face.

'Now, I know what you're all thinking – that the environment controls were deadlocked by Ted...'

'Ted's dead,' gurgled the Nocturn who had been Miss Birch.

'That's true,' the Doctor agreed. 'But the bit about the controls being deadlocked isn't. I lied. Bad habit, I know, but there you are. No one's perfect.'

'Explain!'

'I wasn't trying to find the correct sonic frequency to decode the lock. I was actually setting my screwdriver here to act as a remote control. A light switch.'

Then he held the sonic aloft, pointing it directly up into the sky at the waning moon. The tip of the screwdriver glowed blue. The three Nocturns looked up as one, almost comically alarmed, in time to see the moon suddenly increasing in brightness.

It was as if a giant light bulb had been switched on overhead.

The Nocturns cowered in the instant glare, hissing and seething. The screwdriver's pitch increased and the sun grew even brighter.

Light flooded the grounds, washing away every shadow. The Nocturns began to retreat into their human-shaped shells. But it was too late. One by one, the Nocturns collapsed. The one who had been disguised as Miss Birch, glowered up at the Doctor and spoke in a subdued, rasping voice:

'So you win, Doctor... The game is over.'

Then she, too, sank to the ground.

The Doctor switched off the sonic and returned it to his pocket. Then, squinting up at the blazing sun, he loosened his bow tie and opened his collar. 'Turned out nice again,' he said.

Gisella and Zalenby were running for their lives. They used the parked spacecraft for cover, but the Agent seemed to be able to track them through the landing bays without any difficulty.

The night had turned into day as they ran. For a second they slowed, bewildered and dazzled.

'Hey, who turned on the lights?' asked Zalenby, blinking rapidly.

Gisella looked up at the sun, shielding her eyes. 'I think it's the Doctor. He's the only person I know who could do something like that!'

'Keep going,' Zalenby suddenly urged Gisella on. 'That robot's seen us!'

They ducked under a low-slung cruiser; they had

no idea who it belonged to, but Karl Zalenby knew what kind of ship it was.

'Silenus cruiser,' he said, patting the polished hull. 'I wonder who flew this baby in?'

'Does it matter? They probably won't be flying it out.'

Zalenby pulled Gisella behind one of the landing legs. They could already hear the rhythmic metallic tread of the approaching robot.

'Any attempt to conceal yourselves is pointless,' boomed the Agent. 'I have thermotronic vision. I can trace you via your body heat if necessary. I will find you and kill you.'

'I suppose it means we can run, but we can't hide,' said Gisella.

'And we're running out of hiding places.' Zalenby said. 'What does it want, anyway? I mean, where did it come from? It's not part of the Game of Death, is it?'

'It's a seek-and-destroy machine sent by the Darksmith Collective. It's seeking a special Crystal belonging to them – and it'll destroy the Doctor and me to get it.'

'A Crystal?'

'Long story. You're just an incidental character, I'm afraid.'

'I'd like to stay that way if at all possible.'

'I don't know about that,' Gisella said. 'It may ignore you if it's not programmed to harm you. On the other hand, if you get in the way, it'll kill you without a second's hesitation.'

'Great.' Zalenby peeked out from the side of the landing strut. The Agent stalked into the landing bay, its metal head scanning from side to side.

'It looks a bit battered. If I could get my laser gun...'

'It's suffered extensive damage chasing the Doctor and me through time and space, and the Nocturn damaged its built-in blaster. But it's still utterly lethal and completely unstoppable.'

The Agent suddenly veered in their direction, its glowing eyes fixated on the Silenus cruiser. It raised one arm, pointing its fist at the spacecraft, a tell-tale whine building up somewhere inside the robot.

'Looks like its repaired itself, and it's going to shoot!' yelled Gisella. 'Run!'

A brilliant force-beam erupted from the Agent's fist and slammed into the spaceship. The chromium surface reflected the rays in every direction, throwing off a hundred different coloured beams like a fractured rainbow.

At the edge of the spaceport area, the Doctor

looked up as light beams of every colour shot up into the sky.

'Laser show?' he wondered, frowning. Then realization dawned. 'Oh, no! Not good!'

And he began to sprint towards the glimmering light.

Gisella and Zalenby dashed across the landing bay. The Agent turned, following them with its gun-hand, blasting the concrete as they moved. They dived behind an energy refuelling station as the beam closed in.

The energy station glowed red and then exploded.

On the other side, Gisella and Zalenby were already running, but the blast threw them into the air. Gisella hit the ground heavily and felt a wave of heat pass over her as fiery debris flew all around.

Zalenby lay on his back, dazed. Gisella helped him up, but he could hardly walk. His face was covered in cuts and bruises where fragments from the explosion had hit. There was an ugly gash on his right leg and blood stained his trousers.

Behind them, remorselessly, came the Agent. It walked calmly through the flaming wreckage, its glowing eyes never leaving Gisella.

'Come on, Zalenby!' she urged, pulling him to his feet. She held his hand and ran, half-dragging him behind her.

'It is pointless to run,' repeated the robot. Its metallic voice echoed around the landing bay. 'Failure is not an option.'

Gisella led Zalenby to the next spaceship, a blocky, oily looking vessel standing on three support legs.

'Look,' Zalenby said, pointing past it. 'There's my ship! We're nearly back where we started!'

Gisella saw the gleaming red rocket and shook her head. 'We'll never make it,' she said.

'We'll have to try.'

The robot stomped around the corner. Under the shadow of the spaceship, its eyes glowed like two burning coals. 'Give me the Eternity Crystal,' it ordered, closing in on Gisella.

Moving incredibly fast, Gisella ducked beneath the Agent's outstretched arm. Steel fingers snapped shut on empty air. With an aggravated whirr, the robot turned to follow her.

It had completely ignored Zalenby.

'Big mistake,' he muttered. He may not have been a racing pilot, but he knew his way around spaceships. He reached up and opened an access hatch on the underside of the ship. There were a number of controls inside, but the one he wanted operated the landing gear. It only took a second to override the programming, and then run.

The spaceship immediately began to lower itself down on its stubby legs. Zalenby dived clear, but the Agent had not seen the underside of the vessel descending until several hundred tons of metal pressed down on its head.

The robot twisted, reacting quickly, but not quickly enough. With a screech of metal on metal, it tried to brace itself beneath the ship, raising its arms in an effort to lift it clear. The Agent was strong, but not strong enough. Sparks flew from its joints as the ship continued to lower itself.

The Agent tried to drag itself free, but there was no more room to manoeuvre. The ship forced its way down, squashing the robot beneath it with a terrible, grinding crunch. Its eyes glowed with an insane anger before disappearing completely.

Gisella and Zalenby watched as the ship settled on the concrete. They heard a series of muffled cracks and bangs and then there was silence.

Gisella looked up at the sound of footsteps approaching rapidly.

The Doctor raced around the corner, looking from her to the spaceship and back again.

'What's going on? What've I missed?'

'It was the Agent,' she said. 'It's under there.'

The Doctor looked again at the spacecraft which lay flat on the concrete.

'It'll be no more than scrap now,' said Zalenby.

The Doctor scratched his head. 'Are you sure? That thing's a lot tougher than it looks, and it looks pretty tough. The Darksmiths don't mess around when they make one-offs like that.'

'It's over,' said Gisella. She put her arms around the Doctor. 'Thank goodness you're safe. What happened to the Nocturn?'

'Nocturns,' the Doctor corrected. 'There was a nest of them here, running the Game of Death as a scam. But they won't be bothering anyone for the time being.'

'We'd better get Commander Zalenby back to his ship,' said Gisella. 'He's injured.'

'Commander *who*?'

'Zalenby. He's not really Horatio Hamilton at all. He's an undercover policeman.'

'I was right, everyone's got a secret around here. I told you he couldn't have got here in a day from Altair 59, didn't I? And all that rubbish about him getting ready to leave and being scared...'

'Never mind that now. Help me get him back

to his ship.'

Behind them, something clanged.

'What was that?' Zalenby asked thickly.

'Just the metal settling,' Gisella said.

'I don't think so,' said the Doctor.

Then, with a series of crashes and thumps, the ship began to shake and rattle. Then the hull burst open like a steel flower, a huge dent appearing in the metal as something punched through it from the inside. A long, powerful arm broke out, then another and with a metallic tearing sound, the Agent pulled itself free.

'You will give me the Eternity Crystal,' it rasped. Its booming voice sounded strained but determined as it strode towards them. 'You cannot stop me!'

End Game

The robot was damaged. It no longer stood properly upright, but instead walked with a stooping, simian gait. The transparent panels in its body were cracked or missing, exposing the machine beneath, and sparks flew from its joints as it moved.

It limped towards the Doctor, Gisella and Zalenby, who all stared back at the robot in disbelief.

'It's incredible,' said Gisella.

'Beautiful piece of work,' the Doctor admitted. 'Exceptional.'

'Can we stop admiring it and run?' said Zalenby. He turned and began to jog back towards his ship, limping himself.

The Agent's single remaining eye glowed fiercely. It raised its arm, pointing at Gisella. 'You have the

Eternity Crystal,' it said. 'Give it to me or die.'

A whine of energy built up in the robot's gun hand, but when it tried to fire, there was nothing but an angry, harmless clicking.

'Energy ray projector malfunctioning,' it said. Its voice was a slurred rasp, like a piece of rusty metal being dragged across concrete.

'Come on,' said the Doctor, pulling Gisella after him. They caught up with Zalenby by his spaceship.

The robot continued after them. 'Give me the Eternity Crystal,' it ordered. 'Failure is not an option.'

Zalenby bent down beneath his ship and picked up the laser pistol he'd dropped earlier. He checked the charge and then straightened up.

'What are you doing?' Gisella asked.

'I'm going to stop that thing once and for all,' he said, limping back towards the approaching machine. He stopped before the robot and levelled his laser gun.

'Won't work,' said the Doctor.

'Stop where you are or I'll shoot,' warned Zalenby. 'Galactic Police.'

The robot continued to advance. Zalenby fired. A bright red pulse of energy hit the Agent in the chest, sparks flying. It barely slowed. Zalenby had time to squeeze off one more shot before the robot was on him, tearing the laser pistol out of his hand.

The Agent held up the gun and crushed it like paper. Then, brushing Zalenby aside, it continued towards Gisella and the Doctor.

'Give me the Eternity Crystal.'

The Doctor stepped in front of Gisella. 'You'll have to go through me first.'

'Obviously.' The Agent pushed the Doctor to one side. The Doctor flew through the air and smashed into the nearby energy generator.

The Agent loomed over Gisella. 'Give me the Eternity Crystal!'

'Never.' Gisella met the inevitable swing of the robot's giant fist with her forearm. There was a sickening clang, but the blow was deflected. The robot tried again, lashing at her with its other hand, but Gisella blocked that as well.

The Agent paused, calculating.

'I'm an android too,' Gisella explained. She held up her hands, and where the robot's blows had struck her forearms there was a wound in her skin exposing the pneumatic bones and circuitry beneath.

Then she pulled back her fist and punched the Agent hard in the face. It staggered back, sparks jetting from its silver skull. When the next attack came, it reacted quickly enough to defend itself, crossing its forearms to protect its head from a rain of blows. But having raised its arms in this defensive gesture, it exposed itself to a low kick. Gisella's foot lashed out and she spun, straightening her leg, thrusting a heel deep into its midriff. The plastic cracked and the robot doubled up, groaning. Oily smoke began to pour from its innards as interior circuits blew.

Gaining confidence, Gisella moved in. She had never used her full strength and speed before, always adopting the same level of physicality as a human girl of her apparent age. But now, against this wretched thing, she could really cut loose.

But the Agent wasn't finished yet. It had been designed and built by the finest minds of the Darksmith Collective, made from components salvaged, stolen and adapted from the best across the cosmos. Its hand flashed out, grabbing Gisella by the throat. Heavy steel fingers began to squeeze, closing with the inexorable power of a vice. Within moments those fingers would scissor right through her neck, decapitating her.

Gisella's eyes widened in fear. She struggled, but,

as damaged as it was, the robot was still too strong. It always had been.

The Agent's single remaining eye glowed fiercely.

And then it suddenly flickered.

The robot began to shake, energy crackling around it, surging up through the electronics inside it and then bursting from the holes in its skull like fire. Its fingers flexed as it lost control of all motor functions and Gisella fell to the floor. She looked up and saw the robot transfixed, arms and legs rigid, as lightning scoured the armour plating and ripped the machine wide open.

The Doctor crawled over and pushed the nozzle of the energy generator's hose deep into the robot's exposed innards.

At last, the metal and plastic shredded almost beyond recognition. What remained of the Agent fell forward and crashed to the floor, breaking up into a series of mechanical parts, twisted and useless.

Gisella crawled across to the wreckage. The Agent's head, cracked and dented and charred, rolled to one side. Its eyes glowed faintly as it looked up at her.

'I'm sorry,' she whispered.

'Failure... is not... an option...' The robot made a final, inarticulate whirr and then the green glow in its eye faded forever.

'It's gone,' said the Doctor. There was a note of sadness in his voice. 'It was an incredible machine. There will never be another one like it.'

Gisella closed her eyes. 'Thank goodness.'

Later, in the TARDIS, Gisella watched the Doctor connect a tiny component he'd taken from the Agent's shattered skull to the control console. The light from the time machine's inner workings cast a green glow across his face as he worked.

'What's that?' Gisella asked.

'You could say I'm picking the robot's brains,' said the Doctor, concentrating on the task.

'What for?'

The Doctor peered over his glasses at her. 'You'll see.'

'What will happen to Miss Birch and the others?'

'They're actually wanted criminals. Hamilton – or rather Commander Zalenby – has put a call into the Galactic Police. There's a Judoon ship on its way here already. Knowing them, they'll probably impound Devastation Hall and the asteroid it stands on. And then they'll impose an exclusion zone around this sector of the Silver Devastation. There will be a lot of form-filling too, which is as good a reason as any for us to leave.'

'I liked Zalenby.'

'Yeah, he's one of the good guys all right.' The Doctor glanced at her. 'Like you.'

'But I didn't do anything.'

'Standing up to that robot was incredibly brave,' the Doctor told Gisella. 'I couldn't have stopped it on my own – and it's thanks to you that we've now got this.' He tapped the little electronic component.

'The robot's brain? How will that help us?'

'Well it's more of a computer core matrix than a brain, and it shares some of the same crypto-molecular structure as the Eternity Crystal. Which is exactly what the TARDIS needs to work out a way for us to destroy it.'

'Brilliant!'

'Couldn't have put it better myself,' the Doctor said, flipping the sonic screwdriver and catching it with a flourish. 'There – all done.'

The console pulsed with light and the tiny component sparkled in its nest of wires and circuitry. The Doctor pulled the scanner screen around and tilted it for them both to check the readout.

His face fell. 'Oh dear, that's not good news...'

Gisella watched the hexagonal patterns moving on the screen. She still couldn't work out how to interpret them, but the Doctor was clearly concerned. 'Why? What does it mean?'

'According to the TARDIS, the only people with the power and technology to destroy the Crystal are those who commissioned its creation. A sort of doomsday circuit.'

'And who are they? Who originally commissioned the Darksmiths to create the Eternity Crystal?'

'I haven't a clue. But there is some data embedded deep in this brain that has survived. An appointment, a meeting of some sort. It looks as though a delegation of Darksmiths recently met with their mysterious clients to discuss the Eternity Crystal. Probably when they realized it had resurfaced. The co-ordinates refer to a particular planet.'

'Which is?'

The Doctor stared at the screen, his face grim. 'Ursulonamex. Otherwise known as Oblivion.'

'That doesn't sound very nice.'

'No,' agreed the Doctor. 'But you'd be surprised.'

He looked thoughtful for a few seconds and then suddenly grinned at her. 'So what are we waiting for?'

And then he threw the lever that would send the TARDIS hurtling through time and space – towards Oblivion.

To Be Continued...

To find out what events lie in store
for the Doctor and the mystery of the
Darksmith Legacy, look out for
The Planet of Oblivion.
But for now, here is a taste of
things to come....

BBC

DOCTOR · WHO

Book
7

THE DARKSMITH LEGACY
THE PLANET OF OBLIVION

BY JUSTIN RICHARDS

www.thedarksmithlegacy.com

Continue the amazing adventure online

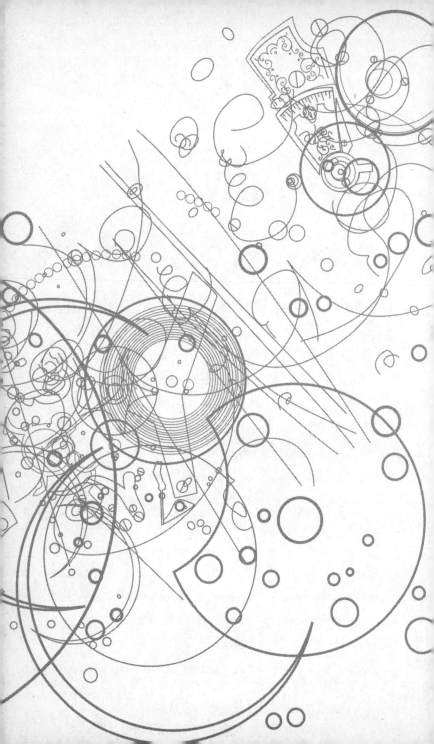

Arrival

'Won't take long,' the Doctor assured Gisella. 'Well, I say it won't take long. But long doesn't actually mean anything when we're travelling in the TARDIS. Or short. Or quick or slow or just about ten minutes more or less.'

Gisella laughed. Although she was a robotic android created by the Darksmith Varlos, she looked like a young girl, perhaps eleven years old. She had a very round, pale and delicate face with big, dark eyes and black hair cut in a perfect bob.

Varlos had used the same technology that had created the Eternity Crystal, which the Darksmiths were so desperate to recover, to give Gisella life. She was much more than a robot. For one thing, the Doctor thought, she could laugh.

'I have no idea what you're on about Doctor,'

Gisella said. 'You talk such rubbish sometimes. Why can't you just say what you mean?'

And she could be a bit annoying too – rubbish?! The Doctor sighed. 'I mean, that it might not seem like it, but we'll be there in the blink of an eye. A moment after leaving Devastation Hall behind, we'll arrive on Ursulonamex.'

The central column of the TARDIS was rising and falling rhythmically. The sound of the time machine's powerful engines cut through the control room – a rasping, grating noise.

'In fact, here we are,' the Doctor said, running round the console and checking the controls. He paused, frowning as he examined a readout. He picked up a large hammer he kept handy for just this sort of thing, and thumped it down hard on the console. 'There, that's better.'

'Are we there?' Gisella asked.

The Doctor grinned massively. 'Welcome to the Planet of Oblivion.' He reached for the door control.

'So why's it called the Planet of Oblivion?' Gisella asked.

It was almost dark in the forest. But Gisella's electronic eyes immediately adjusted to the low light. Patches of pale sunlight broke through the